and found
his dinner
wherever he could.

He liked to bark at
the huge blue things
that thundered past . . .

...and to run in the **big green place** where he saw lots of other dogs.
The other dogs all had people to take for walks.
He wished he had a person, too.

Sometimes, he tried to join in the other dogs' games, but their people called him "fleabag!" and told him to "shoo!"

Then one day he saw a boy with a ball,
but no dog. The boy's big person was busy,
and he had no one to play with.
That didn't seem right.

So when the boy threw his ball,
the dog ran as fast as he could...

across the green stuff...

through the pink things...

and caught it!

That was fun.
He'd never done playing before.

The boy looked very pleased.
He tickled the dog under the chin.
The dog liked that.
He'd never been tickled before.

"Don't touch him, Bob!"
said the boy's big person.
"He's all mucky."

"I don't mind," said Bob.
"I like him."

Over the next few days
the dog looked out for his boy,

and the boy looked out for his dog.

The boy's big person
was usually too busy to notice,

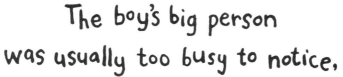

and they became great friends.

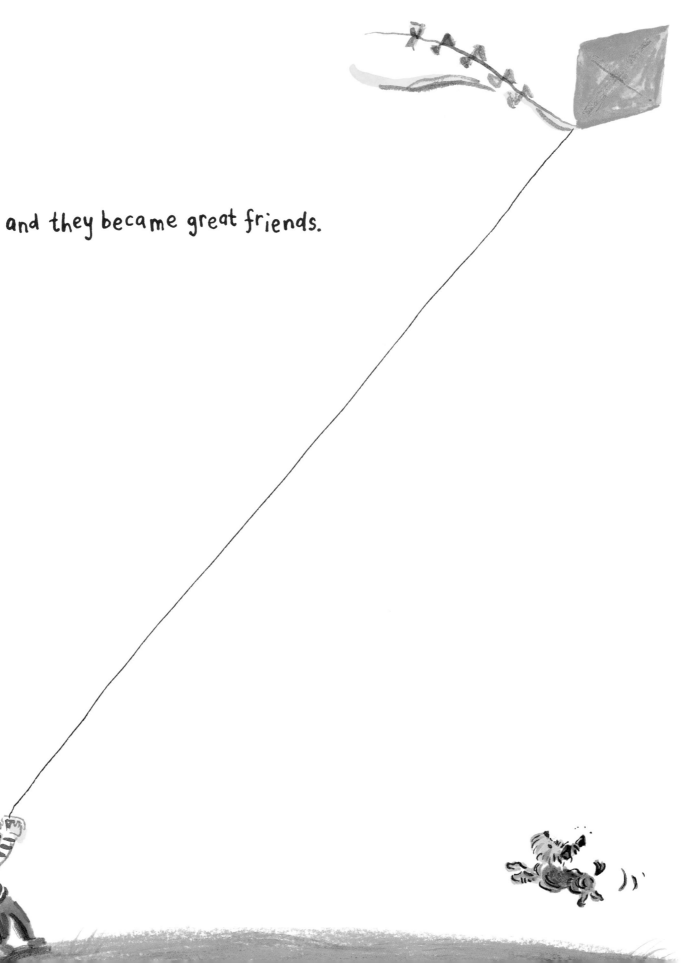

But then one day, the boy didn't feel like playing.
He was too sad.

He told the dog that his family were moving house
the next day. They were going far away, and he
wouldn't be able to play with the dog ever again.

The dog waggled his eyebrows
as if he understood, but he didn't really.

Then the boy's big person called out, "Come on, Bob! Home time! Leave that little fleabag alone, now."

"I have to go with my mum," said the boy.

"I'll miss you," and he shook the dog's paw.

Then the boy followed his mum . . . and the dog followed his boy . . .
all the way home.

That night,
the boy couldn't sleep.
When he looked out of his window,
he could see his dog sitting far below.

"I can't leave you behind," he thought —
and he decided to do something very scary.

He picked up his suitcase which was already packed
for the move, stuffed a few biscuits in his pocket,
and tiptoed out of the flat.

He was scared as he scampered down the stairs.

He was scared as the heavy door shut behind him.

He was scared as he
ran to meet his friend.

"Come on, boy!" he said, bravely.
"We're running away!"

The dog was very confused.
What was his boy doing outside in the dark?
He should be safe indoors with his big people.
He sat very still.

"Come on!"
said the boy.
But the dog wouldn't move.

"Biscuit?"
said the boy.
But the dog wouldn't budge.

"I'll just have to carry you," said the boy, but the dog wriggled free and tried to pull his boy back home.

Then he ran round and round him, barking.

"Shush!"
said the boy.
"You'll wake
up Mum and Dad!"
That seemed like a good
idea, so the dog went:

WOO

WOOF!

woof!

WOOF!

W

Woof!

woof!

WOOF!

woof!

WOOF!

Woof!

woof!

Woof!

Woof!

oof!

WOOF!

Woof!

WOOF!

. . . until a light went on,
and a worried face looked out.

The boy's big people seemed rather cross.
They sent him straight back to bed.

Then one of them said,
"I suppose this little fleabag can sleep here tonight."
"I think he deserves to," said the other.
"He did look after Bob."

The dog was very excited.
He'd never slept in a real bed before.

The next day, the family took everything
out of their flat and put it in an enormous van.
Then, when the van was full, they got into their car.
The dog was worried. Were his people going
somewhere without him?

Then the man said,
"Come on, little fleabag! Hop in!
You're coming with us."

And that's how the dog with
no name found a home!

The dog soon settled in.

Dad got rid of his fleas,
which was good.

Mum got him nice and clean,
which wasn't so good.

Then Bob got him nice
and dirty all over again.

The dog listened while his family tried to think of a name for him.

"Scruff?" said Mum.

"Ga-ga?" said the baby.

"Spike?" said Dad.

But the only name that stuck . . .

was Fleabag!

Fleabag was inspired by
a dog I met at Battersea
Dogs' Home, a special place
for dogs who need new homes. His name
was Fynn, he had lovely bushy eyebrows and
seemed to enjoy being drawn. These are some of the
sketches I did. The day I met him he had found a new home
and was freshly shampooed waiting for his new big people
to collect him.

This book is dedicated to all the dogs at Battersea Dogs' Home.

*Helen Stephens*

Black ears
Black

First published in 2008 by
Alison Green Books
An imprint of Scholastic Children's Books
Euston House, 24 Eversholt Street
London NW1 1DB
A division of Scholastic Ltd
www.scholastic.co.uk
London – New York – Toronto – Sydney – Auckland
Mexico City – New Delhi – Hong Kong

Copyright © 2008 Helen Stephens

HB ISBN: 978 1 407105 63 5
PB ISBN: 978 1 407105 93 2

Black fur
light Brown face &
legs & paws

Fynn Battersea Dogs' Home 21/4/06